Written by
SCOTT SONNEBORN

Illustrated by
OMAR LOZANO

THE NORTH POLICE

Computer Meltdown

RAINTREE

D0582405

Raintree is an imprint of Capstone Global Library Limited,
a company incorporated in England and Wales having its registered office at
7 Pilgrim Street, London, EC4V 6LB – Registered company number: 6695582

www.raintree.co.uk
myorders@raintree.co.uk

Text © Scott Sonneborn 2016
Illustrations © Capstone Global Library Limited 2016
The moral rights of the proprietor have been asserted.

ISBN: 978 1 4747 0032 0

19 18 17 16 15
10 9 8 7 6 5 4 3 2 1

British Library Cataloguing in Publication Data
A full catalogue record for this book is available from the British Library.

Designer: Bob Lentz

Printed in China.

CONTENTS

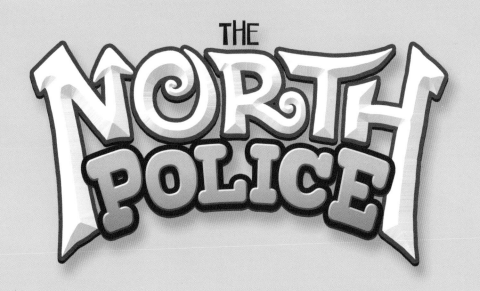

THE NORTH POLICE

The North Police are

the elves who solve crimes

at the North Pole.

These are their stories...

CHAPTER 1
Santa's computer

Inside Santa's workshop

was a computer. Every day,

Santa sat at this computer.

Every day, he added names to

his naughty and nice lists.

But not today...

Santa's computer was
missing!

"It was here yesterday,"
Santa told the North Police's
two greatest detectives. "Now
there's just a puddle."

"Christmas is tomorrow," said Santa sadly. "How will I know who should get presents without my lists? You've got to find out what's happened to my computer!"

 "Maybe the computer had a meltdown," said Detective Sprinkles. "It is rather warm in here."

"I've never heard of a computer melting into water," said Detective Sugarplum. "But there's one way to find out if that's what happened."

"To the lab!" Sprinkles said.

The North Police scooped

the water into a sandwich bag.

"To all a good night of

crime solving!" exclaimed

Santa as the North Police left.

CHAPTER 2
The North Police's lab

At the lab, Sprinkles and Sugarplum waited. Their helper elf tested the water.

First, he poured the water into a test tube. Then he put it under a microscope.

A minute later, the helper
took off his safety goggles
and read the results.

"This is water," he said.

"Computer water?" asked

Detective Sprinkles.

"No, water water," the elf
explained. "Melted snow."

The helper lifted the test
tube to his mouth. He drank
every last drop.

"Melted snow!" shouted
Detective Sugarplum. "Let's
take another look at the
crime scene, Sprinkles. I think
I might know what happened
to Santa's computer!"

CHAPTER 3
Cold case

The two North Police

detectives returned to the

scene of the crime.

"Look," said Sugarplum,

pointing to the floor. "There's

more water over here."

"So?" replied Sprinkles. "It's just melted snow."

"Exactly!" said Detective Sugarplum. "And look where it leads..."

The puddles of water led directly to the toilet blocks. There were three toilet blocks: the women's, the men's and the snowmen's.

WHAM! WHAM! Detective Sugarplum knocked on the door to the snowmen's block.

"Open up!" she said. "It's the North Police!"

There was no answer.

"If there's a snowman in there, button up your coal buttons," said Sugarplum. "We're coming in!"

The two elves burst into

the snowmen's block.

"Brrr," said Sprinkles.

"This isn't like any other

toilet block I've ever seen."

"That's because you're not a snowman," said a voice.

The two North Police detectives turned and saw a snowman. He was holding Santa's computer!

"How did you know I took

it?" asked the snowman.

"The melted snow," said

Detective Sugarplum. "That's

what gave you away."

The snowman nodded.

"It was so hot in Santa's workshop that I started to melt," the snowman said. "So I grabbed the computer and brought it here."

"I knew taking the computer was wrong, but I did it anyway," the snowman said. "I just had to find out if my name was on Santa's list!"

"Well, you're definitely on Santa's list now," said Detective Sprinkles.

"Really?" asked the snowman. "Naughty or nice?"

Sugarplum handcuffed the snowman. "I'll let you work that out," she said.

The North Police smiled.

"Another case neatly wrapped up!" they cheered.

CASE CLOSED!

2.2
2.0
1.8
1.6
1.4
1.2
1.0
0.8

CASE 001   NORTH POLICE
CLANCY
Snowman • Height 2.1 m • Weight 113 kg

GLOSSARY

clue something that helps you find an answer to a question or mystery

detective someone who investigates crimes

microscope instrument with powerful lenses used to make small things appear larger

naughty badly behaved or not following rules

test tube glass tube that is closed at one end and used in science experiments

These are their stories...

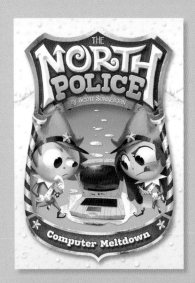

Computer Meltdown

Meet the South Police

The Mystery of Santa's Sleigh

Reindeer Games

only from RAiNTREE!

AUTHOR

Scott Sonneborn has written many books, a circus (for Ringling Bros. Barnum & Bailey) and lots of TV programmes. He's been nominated for one Emmy and spent three amazing years working at DC Comics. He lives in Los Angeles, USA, with his wife and their two sons.

ILLUSTRATOR

Omar Lozano lives in Monterrey, Mexico. He has always been crazy about illustration, constantly on the lookout for awesome things to draw. In his spare time, he watches lots of films, reads fantasy and sci-fi books and draws! Omar has worked for Marvel, DC, IDW, Capstone and many other publishers.